The Solar M

S. P. Meek

Alpha Editions

This edition published in 2023

ISBN : 9789357968713

Design and Setting By
Alpha Editions
www.alphaedis.com
Email - info@alphaedis.com

The Solar Magnet

By Capt. S. P. Meek

THE milling crowd in front of the Capitol suddenly grew quiet. A tall portly figure came out onto the porch of the building and stepped before a microphone erected on the steps. A battery of press cameras clicked. A newsreel photographer ground away on his machine. Wild cheers rent the air. The President held up his hand for silence. As the cheering died away he spoke into the microphone.

"My countrymen," he said, "the Congress of the United States has met in extraordinary session and is ready to cope with the condition with which we are confronted. While they deliberate as to the steps to be taken, it is essential that you meet this danger, if it be a danger, with the bravery and the calm front which has always characterized the people of the United States in times of trial and danger. You may rest assured—"

A slightly built, inconspicuous man who had followed the President out onto the porch was surveying the crowd intently. He turned and spoke in an undertone to a second man who mysteriously appeared from nowhere as the first man spoke. He listened for a moment, nodded, and edged closer to the President. The first man slipped unobtrusively down the Capitol steps and mingled with the crowd.

"—that no steps will be neglected which may prove of value," went on the President. "The greatest scientists of the country have gathered in this city in conference and they undoubtedly will soon find a simple and natural explanation for what is happening. In the meantime—"

THE President paused. From the crowd in front of him came a sudden disturbance. A man sprang free of the crowd and broke through the restraining cordon of police. In his hand gleamed an ugly blue steel automatic pistol. Quickly he leveled it and fired. A puff of dust came from the Capitol. The bullet had landed a few inches from one of the lower windows, fifty feet from where the President stood. He raised his weapon for a second shot but it was never fired. The man who had come down the Capitol steps sprang forward like a cat and grasped the weapon. For a moment the two men struggled, but only for a moment. From the crowd, stunned for a moment by the sheer audacity of the attack, came a roar of rage. The police closed in about the struggling men but the crowd rolled over them like a wave. The captor shouted his identity and tried to display the gold badge of the secret service but the mob was in no state of mind to listen. The police were trampled underfoot and the would-be assassin torn from the hands of the secret service operative. Every man in reach tried to strike a blow. The secret service man was buffeted and thrown aside. Realizing that the affair had been taken out of his hands, he made his way to the rear of the Capitol where his badge gained him ready passage through the cordon of police. He entered the building and reappeared in a few moments by the side of the President.

TWO hours later he leaned forward in his chair in Dr. Bird's private laboratory in the Bureau of Standards and spoke earnestly.

"Dr. Bird," he said, "that bullet was never meant for the President. That man was after bigger game."

The famous scientist nodded thoughtfully.

"Even a very rotten pistol shot should have come closer to him," he replied. "He must have missed by a good forty feet."

"He missed by a matter of inches. Doctor, that bullet struck the Capitol only two inches from a window. In that window was standing a man. The bullet was intended for the occupant of that window. I was directly behind him when he raised his weapon for a second shot and I am sure of his aim. He deliberately ignored the President and aimed again at that window. That was when I tackled him."

"Who was standing there, Carnes?"

"*You* were, Doctor."

Dr. Bird whistled.

"Then you think that bullet was intended for me?"

"I am sure of it, Doctor. That fact proves one thing to me. You are right in your idea that this whole affair is man-made and not an accident of nature. The guiding intelligence back of it fears you more than he fears anyone else and he took this means to get rid of you unobtrusively. Attention was focused on the President. Your death would have been laid to accident. It was a clever thought."

"It does look that way, Carnes," said the doctor slowly. "If you are right, this incident confirms my opinion. There is only one man in the world clever enough to have disturbed the orderly course of the seasons, and such a plan for my assassination would appeal to his love of the dramatic."

"You mean—"

"Ivan Saranoff, of course."

"We are pretty sure that he hasn't got back to the United States, Doctor."

"You may be right but I am sure of nothing where that man is concerned. However, that fact has no bearing. He may be operating from anywhere. His organization is still in the United States."

A knock sounded at the door. In response to the doctor's command a messenger entered and presented a letter. Dr. Bird read it and dropped it in a waste basket.

"Tell them that I am otherwise engaged just now," he said curtly. The messenger withdrew. "It was just a summons to another meeting of the council of scientists," he said to Carnes. "They'll have to get along without me. All they'll do anyway will be to read a lot of dispatches and wrangle about data and the relative accuracy of their observations. Herriott will lecture for hours on celestial mechanics and propound some fool theory about a hidden body, which doesn't exist, and its possible influence, which would be nil, on the inclination of the earth's axis. After wasting four hours without a single constructive idea being put forward, they will gravely conclude that the sun rose fifty-three seconds earlier at the fortieth north parallel than it did yesterday and correspondingly later at the fortieth south parallel. I know that without wasting time."

"Was it fifty-three seconds to-day, Doctor?"

"Yes. This is the twentieth of July. The sun should have risen at 4:52, sixteen minutes later than it rose on June twentieth and fifty-three seconds later than it rose yesterday. Instead it rose at 4:20, sixteen minutes *earlier* than it did on June twentieth and fifty-three seconds earlier than yesterday."

"I don't understand what is causing it, Doctor. I have tried to follow your published explanations, but they are a little too deep for me."

"AS to the real underlying cause, I am in grave doubts, Carnes, although I can make a pretty shrewd guess. As to the reason for the unnatural lengthening of the day, the explanation is simplicity itself. As you doubtless know, the earth revolves daily on its axis. At the same time, it is moving in a great ellipse about the sun, an ellipse which it takes it a year to cover. If the axis of rotation of the earth were at right angles to the plane of its orbit; in other words, if the earth's equator lay in the plane of the earth's movement about the sun, each day would be of the same length and there would be no seasons. Instead of this being the case, the axis of rotation of the earth is tipped so that the angle between the equator and the elliptic is $23\frac{1}{2}°$."

"I seem to remember something of the sort from my school days."

"This angle of tilt may be assumed to be constant, for I won't bother with the precessions, nutations and other minor movements considered in accurate computations. As the earth moves around the sun, this tilt gives rise to what we call the sun's declination. You can readily see that at one time in the year, the north pole will be at its nearest point to the sun, speaking in terms of tilt and not in miles, while at another point on the elliptic, it will be farthest from the sun and the south pole nearest. There are two midway points when the two poles are practically equidistant."

"Then the days and nights should be of equal length."

"They are. These are the periods of the equinoxes. The point at which the sun is nearest to the south pole we call the winter solstice, and the opposite point, the summer solstice. The summer solstice is on June twenty-first. At that time the declination of the sun is $23\frac{1}{2}°$ north of the equatorial line. It starts to decrease until, six months later, it reaches a minus declination of $23\frac{1}{2}°$ and is that far south of the line. The longest day in the northern hemisphere is naturally June twenty-first."

"And the shortest day when the sun has the greatest minus declination."

"PRECISELY, at the winter solstice. Now to explain what is happening. The year went normally until June twenty-first. That day was of the correct length, about fourteen hours and fifty minutes long. The twenty-second should have been shorter. Instead, it was longer than the twenty-first. Each day, instead of getting shorter as it should at this time of year, is getting longer. We have already gained some thirty-two minutes of sunlight at this latitude. The explanation is that the angle between the equator and the elliptic is no longer $23\frac{1}{2}°$ as it has been from time immemorial, but it is greater. If the continuing tilt keeps up long enough, the obliquity will be 90°. When that happens, there will be perpetual midday at the north pole and perpetual night at the south pole. The whole northern hemisphere will be bathed in a continuous flood of sunlight while the southern hemisphere will be a region of cold and dark. The condition of the earth will resemble that of Mercury where the same face of the planet is continually facing the sun."

"I understand that all right, but I am still in the dark as to what is causing this increase of tilt."

"No more than I am, old dear. Herriott keeps babbling about a hidden body which is drawing the earth from its normal axial rotation, but the fool ignores the fact that a body of a size sufficient to disturb the earth would throw every motion of the solar system into a state of chaos. Nothing of the sort has happened. Ergo, no external force is causing it. I am positive that the force which is doing the work is located on the earth itself. Furthermore, unless my calculations are badly off, this force is located on or very near the surface of the earth at approximately the sixty-fifth degree of north latitude."

"How can you tell that, Doctor?"

"It would take me too long to explain, Carnes. I will, however, qualify my statement a little. Either a variable force is being used or else a constant force located where I have said. The sixty-fifth parallel is a long line. The exact location and the nature of that force, we have to find. If it be man-made, and I'll bet my bottom dollar that it is, we will also have to destroy it. If we fail, we'll see this world plunged into such a riot of war and bloodshed as has never before been known. It will be literally a fight of mankind for a place in the sun. Due to its favorable location in the new position of the earth, it is more than probable that Russia would emerge as the dominant power."

"Undertaking to destroy a thing that you don't know the location of and of whose existence you aren't even sure is a pretty big contract."

"WE'VE tackled bigger ones, old dear. We have the President behind us. I haven't made much headway selling my idea to that gang of old fossils who call themselves the council of scientists, but I did to his nibs. Just before that attempt at assassination, I had a chin-chin with him. The fastest battle cruiser in the Navy, the *Denver*, is to be placed at my service. It will carry a big amphibian plane, so be equipped to assemble and launch it. Bolton will relieve you from the Presidential guard to-day. We sail in the morning."

"Where for, Doctor?"

"I feel sure that the force is caused and controlled by men and I know of but one man who has the genius and the will to do such a thing. That man is Saranoff. Because he must be concealed and work free from interruption, I fancy he is working in his own country. Does that answer your question?"

"It does. We sail for Russia."

"Carnesy, old dear, at times you have flashes of such scintillating brilliance that I have hopes for the future of the secret service. In time they may even show human intelligence. Toddle along now and pay your fond farewells to the bright lights of Washington. Meet me at the Pennsy station at six. We'll sail from New York in the morning."

WITH the famous scientist and his assistant as passengers, the *Denver* steamed at her best speed across the Atlantic. As soon as New York harbor was cleared, Dr. Bird charted the course. Captain Evans raised his eyebrows when he saw the course laid out, but his orders had been positive. Had Dr. Bird ordered him to steam at full speed against the shore, he would have obeyed without question.

The *Denver* avoided the usual lanes of traffic and bore to the north of the summer lane. Not a vessel was sighted in the eight days which elapsed before the Faroe Islands came in sight on the starboard bow. The *Denver* bore still more to the north and skirted around North Cape five days later. At Cape Kanin she headed south into the White Sea. Surprisingly little ice was encountered. When Captain Evans mentioned this, Dr. Bird pointed out to him that it was August and that the days were still lengthening. Once in the White Sea, the *Denver* was made ready for instant action. A huge amphibian plane was hoisted in sections from the hold and mechanics started to assemble it. Dr. Bird spent most of his time working on some instruments he had assembled in the radio room.

"This is an ultra-short wave detector," he explained to Carnes. "It will receive vibrations to the lowest limit of waves that we have ever been able to measure. The X-ray is high on the scale and even the cosmic ray is far above its lower limit of detection. We are hunting for an electro-magnet, the largest and strangest electro-magnet that has ever been constructed. Perhaps it would be more accurate to say that we are seeking for a generator of magnetic force. It does not generate the ordinary magnetism which attracts iron and steel, nor the special type of magnetism which we call gravity, but something between the two. It attracts the sun enough to disturb the tilt of the earth's axis, but not enough to pull the earth out of its orbit. Such a device should give out a wave that can be detected, if we get a receiver delicate enough and operating on the right wave length."

HE spent hours improving and refining the apparatus, but in the end he confessed himself beaten.

"It's no use, Carnes," he said the day after Cape Kanin faded from view to the north. "Either the apparatus we are seeking gives out no wave that we can detect or my apparatus is faulty. Luckily we have other things to guide us."

"What are they, Doctor?"

"The facts that Saranoff must have easy transportation and a source of power. The first precludes him from locating his station far from the sea-coast and the second indicates that it will be near a river or other source of power. The only Russian points on the sixty-fifth parallel that are open to water transport are the Gulf of Anadyr, north of Kamchatka, and the vicinity of Archangel. I passed up Kamchatka because it would mean too long a haul through unfriendly waters from Leningrad and because there is not much water power. Archangel is easy of access at this time of the year and it has the Dwina river for power. That will be our first line of search."

"We will explore by plane, of course?"

"Certainly. We wouldn't get far on foot, especially as neither of us speaks Russian. We'll head south for another day and then— What's that?"

HE paused and listened. From the distance came a dull drone of sound which brought him to his feet with a start. He raced out onto deck with Carnes at his heels. Far overhead in the blue, a tiny speck of black hovered.

"We're on the right trail, Carnes," he said grimly. The plane passed over them. In huge circles it sank toward the ground. Dr. Bird turned to Captain Evans. Orders flew from the bridge and a detail of marines rapidly stripped the covers from the two forward anti-aircraft rifles.

"I dislike to fire on that craft before it makes a hostile demonstration, Dr. Bird," demurred Captain Evans. "We are at peace with Russia. My action in firing might precipitate a war, or in any event, serious diplomatic misunderstandings."

"Allow me to correct you, Captain Evans, we are at war with Russia. The whole world is at war with the man who has pulled the earth out of her course. In any event, your orders are positive and the responsibility is mine. Wait until that plane gets within easy range and then shoot it down. Do not fail to get it; it must not get back to shore with word of our approach."

Captain Evans bowed gravely. Shells came up from the magazines and were piled by the guns. From the fire control stations came a monotonous calling of firing data. The guns slowly changed direction as the plane descended. Nearer and nearer it came, intent on positive identification of the war vessel below it. It passed over the *Denver* less than five thousand feet up. As it passed it swung off to one side and began to climb sharply. Dr. Bird glanced at the fighting top of the cruiser and swore softly. From the top the stars and stripes had been broken to the breeze.

"Fire at once!" he cried, "and then court-martial the fool who broke out that flag!"

THE two three-inch rifles barked their message of death into the sky. For agonizing seconds nothing happened. The guns roared again. Below and behind the fleeing plane, two puffs of white smoke appeared in the sky. The staccato calls of the observers came from the control station and the guns roared again and again. Now above and now below the Russian plane appeared the white puffs that told of bursting shells, but the plane droned on, unharmed.

"It's away safely," groaned the doctor. "Now the fat *is* in the fire. Saranoff will know in an hour that we are coming. If we had a pursuit plane ready to take off, we might catch him, but we haven't. Oh, well, there's no use in crying over spilt milk. How soon will that amphibian be ready to take off?"

"In twenty minutes. Doctor," replied the Engineering Officer. "As soon as we finish filling the tanks and test the motor, she'll be ready to ramble."

"Hurry all you can. Hang a half dozen hundred-pound bombs and a few twenty-fives on the racks. Lower her over the side as soon as she's ready. Where's Lieutenant McCready?"

"Below, getting into his flying togs, Doctor."

"Good enough. Come on, Carnes, we'll go below and put on our fur-lined panties, too. We'll probably need them."

IN half an hour the amphibian rose from the water. Lieutenant McCready was at the controls, with Carnes and the doctor at the bomb racks. The plane rose in huge spirals until the altimeter read four thousand feet. The pilot straightened it out toward the south. The plane was alone in the sky. For two hours it flew south and then veered to the east, following the line of the Gulf of Archangel. The town came in sight at last.

"Better drop down a couple of thousand, Lieutenant," said Dr. Bird into the speaking tube. "We can't see much from this altitude."

The plane swung around in a wide circle, gradually losing altitude. Carnes and the doctor hung over the side watching the ground below them. As they watched a puff of smoke came from a low building a mile from the edge of the town. Dr. Bird grabbed the speaking tube.

"Bank, McCready!" he barked, "They're firing at us."

The plane lurched sharply to one side. From a point a few yards below them and almost directly along their former line of flight, a burst of flame appeared in the air. The plane lurched and reeled as the blast of the explosion reached it. From other points on the ground came other puffs.

"Get out of here," shouted Dr. Bird. "There must be a dozen guns firing at us. One of them will have the range directly."

From all around them came flashes and the roar of explosions. The plane lurched and yawed in a sickening fashion. Lieutenant McCready fought heroically with the controls, trying to prevent the sideslips which were costing him altitude. Gradually the plane came under control and started to climb. The shells burst nearer as the plane took a straighter course and strove to fly out of the danger zone. Dr. Bird looked at the air-speed meter.

"A hundred and eighty," he shouted to Carnes. "We'll be safely out of range in a minute."

THE bursts were mostly behind them now. Suddenly a blast of air struck them with terrific force. Half a dozen holes appeared in the fabric of the wings. A bit of high explosive shell plowed a way through the after compartment and wrecked the duplicate instrument board. In another moment they were out of range. Lieutenant McCready turned the nose of his plane toward the north.

"We came out of that well," cried Carnes. Dr. Bird dropped the speaking tube which he had held pressed to his ear and smiled grimly at the detective.

"I wish we had," he replied. "Our main gas tank is punctured."

An expression of alarm crossed the detective's face.

"Is it injured badly?" he asked.

"I don't know yet. McCready says that the gauge is dropping pretty rapidly. I'm going to go out and see what I can do."

"Can't I go, Doctor? I'm a good deal lighter than you are."

"You're not as strong or as agile, Carnes, and you haven't the mechanical ability to make the repair. Hand me that line."

He fastened one end of a coil of manila rope which Carnes handed him to his waist, while the detective fastened the other end to one of the safety belt hooks. With a word of farewell, he climbed out of the cockpit and onto a wing. In the pocket of his flying suit he carried a tool kit and repair material. Carnes shuddered as the doctor's figure disappeared under the plane. He snubbed the rope about a seat bracket and held it taut. For ten minutes the strain continued. It slackened at last, and the figure of the doctor reappeared on the wing. Slowly he climbed into the cockpit.

"I've made a temporary repair, Lieutenant," he called into the speaking tube, "and the leakage has stopped. How much gas have we left?"

"Enough for about an hour of flying, including the emergency tank."

"Thunder! No chance to get back to the *Denver*. Better head inland and follow the course of the Dwina. If we can locate the place we are looking for we may be able to drop a few eggs on it before we are washed out. In any event, it will be better to come down on land than on water."

MCCREADY headed the plane south and followed the winding ribbon below him which marked the channel of the Dwina. He kept his altitude well over eight thousand feet. For a few minutes the plane roared along. Without warning the motor sputtered once or twice and died.

"Gas finished?" asked Dr. Bird into the speaking tube.

"No, there is plenty of gas for another forty-five minutes. It acted like a short in the wiring. Maybe another fragment got us that we didn't know about. I can glide to a safe landing, Doctor. Which direction shall I go?"

"It doesn't matter," replied Dr. Bird as he looked over the side. "Wait a minute, it does matter. See that long low building down there with the projection like a tower on top? I'll bet a month's pay that that is the very place we're looking for. Glide over it and let's have a look at it. If I am convinced of it, I'll drop a few eggs on it."

"Right!"

McCready glided on a long slope toward the suspected building. Dr. Bird kept his eye glued to the bomb sight.

"It's suspicious enough for me to act," he cried. "Drop one!"

Carnes pulled a lever and a hundred-pound high explosive bomb detached itself from the plane and fell toward the ground.

"Another!" cried the doctor.

A second messenger of death followed the first.

"Bank around and back over while we give them the rest."

"Right!"

The plane swung around in a wide circle.

"Volley!" cried the doctor. Carnes pulled the master lever and the rest of the bombs fell earthward.

"Now glide to the east, McCready, until you are forced down."

MCCREADY banked the plane and started on a long glide toward the east. Carnes and the doctor watched the falling bombs. The doctor's aim had been perfect. The first bomb released struck the building squarely while the other landed only a few feet away. Instead of the puffs of smoke which they had expected, the bombs had no effect. The volley which Carnes had discharged fell full on the building as harmlessly as had the two pilot shots.

"Were these bombs armed, Lieutenant?" demanded the doctor.

"Yes, sir. I inspected them myself before we took off and they were fused and armed. They had always fused and should have gone off, no matter in what position they landed."

"Well, they didn't. That building is our goal all right. Saranoff would naturally expect an air raid and he has perfected some device which renders a bomb impotent before it lands. How far from the building will you land?"

"A couple of miles, Doctor."

"Get as far as you can. If you can make that line of thicket ahead, we'll take to our heels and hope to hide in it."

"I don't think we'll have much luck, Doctor," said Carnes.

"Why not?"

"Look behind."

Dr. Bird looked back toward the building they had tried to bomb. Across the country, a truck loaded with armed men followed the course of the plane. The plane was gaining slightly on the truck but it was evident that the plane's occupants would have little chance of escaping on foot. Dr. Bird gave a grim laugh.

"We're cornered all right," he said. "If we did elude the men in that truck, we would have a plane after us in no time. You might as well turn back, McCready, and land fairly near the building. We are sure to be captured and our best chance is to have the plane near us. They'll probably patch it up and if we get a chance to escape later, it may be a lifesaver. At any rate, we've lost for the present."

McCready turned the plane again to the west. The truck halted at their new maneuver. As the plane passed over, it turned and again followed them. The ground was approaching rapidly. With a final dip, McCready leveled off and made a landing. The machine rolled to a stop about a mile from the building. The truck was less than three hundred yards away. It came up rapidly and disgorged a dozen men armed with rifles who hurried forward. In the lead was a tall, slight figure who carried no gun. Dr. Bird stepped forward to meet them.

"Do you understand English?" he asked.

An incomprehensible jargon of Russian answered him. The men raised their rifles threateningly. Dr. Bird turned back to his companions.

"Resistance is hopeless," he said. "Surrender gracefully and we'll see what comes of it."

He faced the Russians and held one hand high above his head. The Russian leader stepped forward and confiscated the doctor's pistol. He repeated the process with Carnes and McCready, frisking them thoroughly for concealed weapons. At his command, six of the Russians stepped forward. The Americans took their place in the midst of the guard and were marched to the truck. The balance of the Russians moved over to the American's plane. The truck rolled forward and approached the low building. The projection which Dr. Bird had noticed from the air proved to be a metal tube projection from the roof, fully twenty feet in diameter and fifty feet long.

"A projection tube of some sort," said the doctor, pointing. An excited command came from the Russian in command. A rifle was leveled threateningly at the doctor. He took the hint and maintained silence while they climbed down from the truck and approached the door of the building.

It swung open as they approached. As they entered a strong garlic-like smell was evident. The hum of heavy machinery smote their ears.

THEY were led down a corridor to a flight of steps. On the floor below they went along another corridor to a heavy iron-studded door. The guide unlocked it with a huge key and swung it open. With a shrug of his shoulders, Dr. Bird led the way into the cell. The door closed behind them and they were left alone. Dr. Bird turned to his companions.

"Be careful what you say," he whispered. "I am not at all convinced that there is no one here who knows English and we are probably spied upon. There is almost sure to be a dictaphone somewhere in this room. We don't want to give them any more information than we have to."

Carnes and McCready nodded. Dr. Bird spoke aloud of inconsequential matters while they explored the cell. It was a room some twenty feet square, fitted with three bunks on one side, built into the wall like the berths on shipboard. The room was lighted by a single electric light overhead. A door opened into a lavatory equipped with running water.

"We're comfortable here, at any rate," said the doctor cheerfully. "They evidently don't mean to make us suffer. I'd like to know why they took the trouble to capture us, anyway. It would seem to be more in line with their usual policy to have shot us on sight. It must be that they want some sort of information from us."

Neither of his companions had a better reason to offer and conversation languished. For an hour they sat almost without speech. A sound at the door brought them to their feet. It opened and a Russian girl pushed in a cart laden with food. She made no reply to the remarks which Dr. Bird addressed to her but quickly and silently put their food on the table. When she had completed her task, she left the room without having spoken a word.

"Beautiful, but dumb," Dr. Bird remarked. "Let's eat."

"Do you suppose that it's safe to eat this food, Doctor?" asked Carnes in a whisper.

"I don't know, and I don't care. If we've got to go out, we might as well be poisoned as shot. If we refuse food, they can poison us through our water. We couldn't refuse that for any length of time. I'm hungry and I'm going to make a good meal. What's this stuff, *bortsch*?"

THEY soon received proof that they were under observation. Hardly had they pushed back their chairs at the completion of the meal than the door opened and the Russian girl who had brought their food removed the empty dishes. Silence settled down over the cell. For another hour they waited before the door opened again. A tall bearded Russian entered with a younger man at his heels. The bearded man dropped into a chair while his companion sat at the table and opened a notebook.

"Stand up!" barked the Russian sternly.

Carnes and McCready rose to their feet but Dr. Bird remained stretched out on a bed.

"What for?" he demanded languidly.

The Russian bristled with rage.

"When I speak to you, you shall obey," he said in curiously clipped English, "else it will be the worse for you. Would you rather be questioned while in the *strelska* than while standing?"

"Not by a long shot," replied Dr. Bird promptly as he rose to his feet. "Fire away, old fellow. I'll talk."

"What are your names?"

"I am Addison Sims of Seattle," replied Dr. Bird gravely, "and my friends are Mr. Earle Liedermann and Mr. Bernarr Macfadden. You may have read of us in the American magazines."

"Their names," said the Russian to his clerk, "are Dr. Bird, of the Bureau of Standards; Operative Carnes, of the United States Secret Service; and Lieutenant McCready, of the United States Navy. Dr. Bird, you will save yourself trouble if you will answer my future questions truthfully."

"Then ask questions to which I am not sure that you know the answer," replied the doctor dryly.

"What vessel brought you here?"

"The *Denver*."

"What is her armament?"

"Consult the Navy list. You will doubtless find a copy in your files. It may be purchased from the Superintendent of Public Documents at Washington."

"WHAT is your errand here?"

"To consult with Ivan Saranoff and learn his future plans. If he means merely to bestow on the northern hemisphere additional sunshine and warmth, it is possible that the United States will not oppose him. We would benefit equally with Russia, you know. Possibly the northern countries could form some sort of an alliance against the southern hemisphere which is already threatening war."

"You chose a peculiar way of showing your peaceable intentions. You shot down our plane without warning and you dropped bombs on us at first sight."

"But they didn't explode."

"No, thanks to our ray operators. Dr. Bird, I have no time to waste. Either you will answer my questions fully and truthfully or I will resort to torture."

"You don't dare. You were merely bluffing when you mentioned the *strelska*. If you tortured us, you would have to answer to Ivan Saranoff on his return."

"How did you know that he is—" The Russian paused and bit his lip. "Shall I tell him that you refuse to talk?"

"When he returns, you may tell him that I will be glad to talk frankly with him. I came to Russia for that purpose, but I will not talk with one of his underlings. In the meanwhile, we are having lovely weather for this time of year, aren't we?"

With a muttered curse the Russian rose and left the room. Carnes turned to Dr. Bird.

"How did you know that Saranoff was away?" he demanded.

"I didn't," replied Dr. Bird with a chuckle, "it was merely a shrewd guess. We have twisted his tail so often that I figured he could not resist the temptation to come here and gloat a few gloats over us if he were here. I know his ruthless methods in dealing with his subordinates and I knew that they would never dare to resort to torture in his absence. No, old dear, we are safe until he returns. I hope he stays away a long time."

FOUR days passed monotonously. Three times a day the Russian girl appeared with ample meals. Despite their attempts to engage her in conversation, not a word would she reply or give any indication that she either heard or understood their remarks. The bearded Russian appeared daily and tried to question them, but Dr. Bird laughed at his threats and reaffirmed his intention of talking to no one but Saranoff.

"Your chance will soon come," replied the Russian with an evil leer on the fourth day. "He will be here the day after to-morrow. He will be able to make you talk."

"If he's telling the truth, the jig's about up," said Dr. Bird when the Russian had left. "I don't fancy that Saranoff will show us much mercy when he finds out what we've attempted to do."

"How would it be to overpower our waitress and make a break?" asked McCready in a guarded whisper.

"No good at all," replied the doctor decisively. "We wouldn't have a Chinaman's chance. Our best bet is to talk turkey to Saranoff. He may spare us if I can make him believe that I am willing to work for him. What a man he is! If we could turn his genius into the right channels, he would be a blessing to the world."

HE paused as the door swung open and the Russian girl appeared with their food. She placed the cart against the wall and suddenly turned and faced them.

"Dr. Bird," she said in excellent English, "I am Feodrovna Androvitch."

"I'm glad to know you," said Dr. Bird with a bow.

"Do you recognize my name?"

"I'm very sorry, my dear, but it simply doesn't register."

"Do you remember Stefan Androvitch?"

A sudden light came into Dr. Bird's face.

"Yes," he exclaimed, "I do. He used to work for me in the Bureau some time ago. I had to let him go under peculiar circumstances. Is he related to you?"

"He was my twin brother. The peculiar circumstances you refer to were that you caught him stealing platinum. Instead of turning him over to the police, you asked him why he stole. He told you his wife was dying for lack of things that money would buy and he stole for her. You allowed him to quit his position honorably and you gave him money for his immediate needs. For that act of mercy, I am here to reward you."

"Bread cast upon the waters," murmured Carnes. The Russian girl turned on him like a wildcat.

"Unless you wish to deprive yourself and your companions of my help, you will not quote the Bible, that sop thrown by the church to their slaves, to me," she said venomously. "I am a woman of the proletariat!"

"Respect the lady's anti-religious prejudices, Carnesy, old dear," said the doctor with a smile. "How do you propose to aid us, Miss Androvitch?"

"I will give you exactly what you gave my brother, your freedom and money for your immediate needs."

"Thanks. But, er—haven't you considered what your position here will be if you aid us to escape? Saranoff doesn't deal kindly with traitors, I fancy."

The girl spat on the floor.

"That swine!" she hissed, "I would like to kill him. I would have done so long ago had not the hope of the people rested on his genius. When the people finally triumph, I will feed his heart to my cat."

"Nice, gentle, loving disposition," murmured the doctor. "All right, my dear, we're ready for anything. What's the first move?"

THE girl whisked the covers from the food cart and displayed three pistols and belts of ammunition.

"Put these on," she said, "and take this food with you. I will take you to a hiding place outside the walls where you may safely stay for a few days. I will bring you fresh supplies of food. As quickly as possible I will arrange for you to escape from Russia. When you have left Russia safely, my debt is paid and you are again my enemies."

"But, listen here," said Dr. Bird persuasively, "why don't you come with us? You know the object of our coming here. We aim to destroy this plant and let the earth take its normal tilt. You hate Saranoff, although I don't know why. If you'll help us to destroy him, we'll guarantee you a welcome in the United States and you can join your brother. I'll take him back into my laboratory."

"My brother is dead," she said bitterly. "After he left you, he fell into more evil times. His wife died and he swore revenge upon the society which had murdered her. An opportunity came to him to join Saranoff, and he did so. Saranoff hated him and distrusted him, although he was the soul of loyalty. As a reward for his genius and aid to Saranoff in constructing the black lamp, Saranoff abandoned him to you. It was your men who killed him when you blew into nothingness the helicopter he was piloting in your state of Maryland, near Washington."

"All the more reason why you should revenge yourself upon Saranoff," replied the doctor. "We will give you a chance to do so and aid you. We also give you an opportunity to be received in a free country with honor."

An expression of rage distorted the girl's features.

"I am a woman of the proletariat!" she cried. "I hate Ivan Saranoff for what he has done but I am loyal to him. He alone will force the bourgeoisie to their knees and establish the rule of the people. I hate your country and your government; yes, and I hate you. I aid you because I must pay my just debts. Come, the way is clear for your escape. Don't ask how I cleared it."

"Come on," said Dr. Bird with a shrug of his shoulders. "There is no arguing with convictions. She must act according to her lights, even as we must act according to ours. Grab your guns and let's go."

THE three buckled on the weapons and belts of ammunition and followed the girl from the cell. Once outside she touched her lips for silence. A door barred their way but she opened it with a key which she withdrew from her dress. Outside the door, a guard slumbered noisily. At a motion from the girl, Carnes rolled him over on his face to quiet his snoring. He moved and stirred, but did not wake.

A few feet from the door the girl paused and faced the wall. She manipulated a hidden lever and a panel swung open in the wall. She led the way silently into the dark. As the panel closed behind her, a beam of light from an electric torch stabbed the darkness. Down a sloping tunnel they followed her for half a mile. The tunnel turned at right angles and led upward. At length they paused before another door. The girl opened it and they stepped out into the night. As they did so, a dull booming struck their ears. The girl paused.

"The ship!" she cried. "Your ship! It is attacking Fort Novadwinskaja. The factory will be awake in a moment! Run for your lives!"

Even as she spoke a pair of twinkling lights appeared far down the tunnel through which they had come. She turned as if to return down the tunnel. Dr. Bird caught her about the waist and clapped his hand over her mouth.

"Quick, Carnes, your belt," he cried. "Tie her up. She meant to go down that tunnel and give her life to delay them while we escaped. We'll save her in spite of herself."

Carnes and McCready quickly bound the struggling girl with their belts. They laid her on the ground beside the door and watched the oncoming lights.

"You two hold them back for the present," said the doctor. "I'm going to take Feodrovna away a bit and argue gently with her. If I can make her see the light, we may accomplish our mission yet. If I can't, I'll come back and help you."

HE picked up the girl in his arms and disappeared into the darkness. Pistol in hand, the two men watched the oncoming lights. The men behind the lights could not be seen, but from the sound of their footsteps it was evident that there were quite a few of them.

"Had we better let them emerge from the door and then get them?" whispered Carnes.

"No. These heavy guns will drive a bullet through three men at short range. Level your gun down the tunnel and fire when I give the word. Remember, every one is apt to shoot high in the dark."

The lights approached slowly. When they were twenty-five yards away, Lieutenant McCready spoke. The quiet was shattered by the roar of two Luger pistols. Again and again the guns barked. A volley of fire came from the tunnel, but Carnes and the lieutenant were standing well away from the opening and they escaped unharmed. Their deadly fire poured into the shambles until they were rewarded by the sound of retreating feet.

"So ends round one," said Carnes with a laugh. "I think we win on points."

"They won't try a direct attack again," replied the lieutenant. "Look out for a flank attack or from some new weapon. I don't like the way those bombs failed to explode the other day."

Dr. Bird appeared from the darkness.

"McCready," he said in a voice vibrant with excitement, "we're in luck. We have come out less than a hundred yards from the point where our plane came down. It is still there. If the *Denver* has approached within shooting range, we will have enough gas to make it. Try to get your motor going."

"If it isn't completely washed out I'll have it going in a few minutes, Doctor," cried the pilot. "I'm going down the tunnel and get those flash-lights those birds dropped when they pulled out. Where's the girl?"

"She's back by the plane," said the doctor with a chuckle. "She is a spit-fire, all right. I took her gag off and she tried to bite me. I couldn't get a word of anything but abuse out of her. Go ahead and get the lights and I'll show you the plane."

IN a few minutes they stood before the ship. It was apparently uninjured, but the spark was dead. Carnes went back to the tunnel mouth to guard against surprise while Dr. Bird and McCready labored over the motor.

Despite the best of both of them, no spark could be coaxed from the coil. As a last resort, Dr. Bird short-circuited the cells with a screwdriver blade. No answering spark came from the terminals.

"Dead as a mackerel," he remarked. "I guess that ends that hope. Let's get the machine guns out of her. We'll have another attack soon and they'll be more effective than our pistols."

It was the work of a few minutes to dismount the two Brownings from the plane. Carrying the two guns, Dr. Bird joined Carnes while McCready staggered along laden down with belts of ammunition.

"Do you remember that rocky knoll we passed just before we landed?" asked the lieutenant. "If we can get this stuff there before we are attacked, we'll have a much better chance than we will in the open."

"Good idea, Lieutenant. Carnes, connect yourself to one of these guns. I'll fasten the other on my back and carry Feodrovna. We can't leave her here to Saranoff's tender mercies."

Through the night the little cavalcade made its way. The thunder of guns from Fort Novadwinskaja kept up and the sky to the north was lighted by their flashes. McCready's bump of direction proved to be a good one for the sought-for retreat was soon located. As they deposited their burdens and looked back, the lights of two trucks could be seen approaching across the plain from the factory. Hurriedly they mounted the machine gun. Dr. Bird straightened up and listened carefully.

"The guns are sounding less frequently," he said. "Possibly the *Denver* has had enough and is pulling out."

"If I know Captain Evans as well as I think I do, the *Denver* is not retreating," replied McCready grimly.

"I hope she's hammering the fort out of existence," said the doctor. "However, our main interest just now is on the land front. Gunners to the fore. Carnes, you aren't so good at this, better let McCready and me handle them."

THE trucks approached slowly. Presently the American plane loomed up in the glare of their headlights. A powerful searchlight mounted on the leading truck swept the country. Discovery was a matter of moments. Lieutenant McCready trained his gun carefully and pressed the trigger. A rattle of fire came from the Browning. A crash was heard from the truck and the searchlight winked out.

"Bull's-eye!" cried Carnes exultantly.

"Down, you fool!" cried the doctor as he swept the detective from his feet and threw him down behind a rock. His action was none too soon. A burst of machine gun fire came from the trucks and a hail of bullets splattered on the rocks a few yards from them. McCready crawled back to his gun.

"Wait a minute, Lieutenant," counseled the doctor. "A burst of fire from here will give them our location and probably do them little damage. Wait until they try to rush us."

They did not have long to wait. A guttural shout came from a point a few yards away and the sound of running feet came to their ears. The rush was directed toward a point a few yards to the left of where they crouched. Dr. Bird swung his gun around. As the rush passed them, he released his trigger. A volley of screams and oaths from the plain answered the crackle of the Browning. McCready's gun joined in with a staccato burst of fire. The attack could not live before that rain of death. A few running feet were heard from the darkness and a few groans. Presently the roar of a motor came from the direction of the parked trucks. It retreated into the distance and all was quiet.

"Round two goes to us on a knock-down," said Carnes jubilantly. "What will they do next, Doctor?"

"Probably nothing until daylight, now that they know we have machine guns. I wish that we could make that thicket, but it's too far to try. It'll be daylight in an hour or so."

The night was normally short in Archangel at that season of the year and the unnatural lengthening of the day which Saranoff had accomplished made it shorter still. In an hour red streamers in the east announced the approach of daylight. Hardly had they appeared than a dull drone of truck motors came from the direction of the factory.

"Round three is about to commence," announced Carnes. "I wish that I could do something."

"You can as soon as our ammunition runs out, which won't be long," replied McCready. "It will be a matter of pistols at close quarters."

THE trucks approached to within a half mile and stopped. The distance was too great to warrant wasting any of their scanty store of ammunition at such long range. In the dim light they would see the Russians working at the trucks. Presently a flash came from the plain. A whining sound filled the air. With a crash a three-inch shell broke behind them.

"No fun," remarked the doctor. "We'll have to get better cover than this."

A second shell whined through the air and burst over their heads. A third burst a few yards in front of them.

"They have us bracketed now," said McCready. "We'd better slide back a piece before they start rapid fire."

Dragging their prisoner with them, the three men made their way to the reverse side of the knoll. A short search revealed an overhanging ledge under which they crouched in comparative safety from anything but a direct hit above them.

"We're all right here except for the fact that they may rush us under cover of the fire," said the doctor. "One man will have to keep watch all the time and it will be a dangerous detail. I'll take the first hitch."

"You will not!" exclaimed Carnes emphatically. "I have done nothing so far and I am the least important member of the party. I'll do the watching."

"Let's draw straws," suggested McCready. "I'm willing to do that, but if it's a matter of volunteering, I refuse to yield to the civilian branches of the government. The Navy has traditions to uphold, you know."

"McCready's right," replied the doctor. "Get straws, Lieutenant, and we'll draw."

McCready picked up three bits of grass and held them out.

"The shortest goes on watch," he said. Carnes and the doctor drew, McCready exhibited the remaining bit of grass. It was the shortest of the three. He waited until the next shell burst above them and then stepped out from the shelter.

"I'll relieve you in fifteen minutes," said Carnes as he left.

"Right."

WHEN the lieutenant had left, Dr. Bird removed the gag from Feodrovna's mouth and tried to argue with her, but the Russian girl only glared her hatred and refused to talk other than to abuse him. With a sigh, the doctor gave over his efforts and talked to Carnes. The time passed slowly with a constant rain of shells on the knoll.

"It's time for my relief," said Carnes at length. As he spoke the hail of shells on the knoll ceased.

"What the dickens?" cried the doctor.

He and Carnes jumped from their shelter and ran over the knoll. On the plain a few hundred yards from them, a straggling line of Russians were advancing with fixed bayonets. McCready was nowhere in sight.

"Where the devil is McCready?" cried the doctor. "He must have been killed. Hello, one of the guns is gone, too. There's only a belt and a half of ammunition left. I'll try to break that attack up."

He advanced to the gun and trained it carefully. When he pressed the trigger a dull click came from the gun.

"Misfire!" he cried. He drew back the bolt and inserted a fresh cartridge. Again the gun clicked harmlessly. Dr. Bird ejected the shell and examined it. A deep indentation appeared on the primer. Hurriedly he tried a half dozen more cartridges but they refused to explode. He turned a keen gaze toward the trucks. On the ground was set a tube-like projector pointing toward them. Dr. Bird swore softly and jerked his pistol from its holster. The hammer clicked futilely on a cartridge.

"Stymied!" he exclaimed. "They have that portable ray mechanism, with them, which disabled our bombs. It's hand to hand, Carnesy, old dear. I wonder where McCready is."

THE Russians approached slowly, keeping their lines straight. They were within two hundred yards of the knoll. Suddenly from a point a hundred yards to the left of the end of the land came a rattle of fire. The attacking line dropped in a pile of grotesque heaps.

"It's McCready!" shouted Carnes. A little ravine ran from the knoll toward the trucks. Sitting in the ravine was the lieutenant, playing a Browning machine gun on the line of attackers. When there were no more of them on their feet, he turned his gun on the trucks. Panic seized the Russians and they made a rush for their truck. Their leader leaped among them, yelling furiously. They paused and turned to the projector tube. Slowly they swung it around. The lieutenant's gun ceased firing.

As the Russians rushed the now silent gun, Dr. Bird stepped to the gun on the knoll. He trained it and pressed the trigger. A rattle of fire came from it and two of the rushing figures fell. The attack paused for an instant. McCready had risen to his feet and was running up the ravine with his gun under his arm.

"Good head!" cried Dr. Bird, "Clever work! Watch the fun now."

He ceased firing his gun. The Russians wavered and then rushed the point from which McCready had fired. The lieutenant allowed them to get to within a short distance and then crumpled the attack with another burst of fire from the flank. With cries of alarm, the Russians turned and fled toward their trucks. McCready ran along the ravine until he was within fifty yards of the standing machines. As the Russians approached, one of them stepped to the truck crank. McCready's pistol spoke and he dropped. A second shared his fate. With cries of despair, the Russians climbed into the remaining truck whose motor was running. Rapidly it drove away across the plain. McCready rose from the ravine and ran toward the standing truck. He started the motor and headed for the knoll.

"He's got a truck," cried Carnes. "We can get away in it."

"Where to?" demanded Dr. Bird. "Archangel is between us and the *Denver*."

The truck came up.

"Come on, Doctor," cried McCready. "Hurry up. We'll take the battery out of this truck and get our plane going."

"Oh, clever!" cried Dr. Bird admiringly. "Load that gun while I get Feodrovna, Carnesy. We'll get away safely yet."

THE truck rolled up to the plane and stopped. While Carnes transferred the prisoner and the guns to the plane, the lieutenant and Dr. Bird ripped up the floor boards of the truck and exposed the battery. It was a matter of moments to detach it and carry it to the plane. It would not fit in place but they anchored it in place with wire.

"You'd better hurry," cried Carnes. "Here come a couple more trucks over the plain."

"That'll do, Doctor," said McCready. "Get on the prop and we'll see if the old puddle jumper will take off."

Dr. Bird ran to the propeller.

"Ready!" he cried.

"Contact!" snapped McCready.

The plane motor roared into life. The ship moved slowly forward as Dr. Bird climbed on board. Toward the oncoming trucks they rushed across the plain. A crash seemed imminent. In the nick of time McCready pulled back on his joystick and the plane rose gracefully into the air, clearing the leading truck by inches. The truck halted and hastily mounted a machine gun.

"Too late!" laughed the lieutenant. "Now it's our turn for some fun."

He tapped the key of his radio transmitter. In a few seconds he received an answer.

"They have reduced Fort Novadwinskaja," he reported to the rear cockpit, "but they don't know what to fire at next. Their largest guns will reach the factory easily. Shall I start some fireworks?"

"You may fire when ready, Gridly," chuckled Dr. Bird.

Again the lieutenant depressed his key. From their altitude of four thousand feet, they could see the *Denver*. From its forward turret came a puff of smoke. There were a few moments of pause and then a cloud of black rose from the plain below them, half a mile from the factory. McCready reported the position of the burst to the ship. A second shell burst beyond the factory and the third just in front of it.

"It's a clear bracket," said McCready. "Now watch the gun. I'll give them a salvo."

FROM the side of the *Denver* came a cloud of black smoke as all of her turret guns fired in unison. The aim was perfect. For a few moments all was quiet and then the factory disappeared in a smother of bursting high explosive shells.

Hardly had the shells landed than a terrific sheet of lightning ripped across the sky. The thunderclap which seemed to come simultaneously, rocked the plane like a feather. Sheet after sheet of lightning illuminated the sky while the roar of thunder was continuous. Rain fell in solid sheets. Even as they watched, it began to turn into snow. The air grew bitterly cold.

"The solar magnet is wrecked," shouted the doctor, "and these storms are the efforts of nature to return to normal."

"If they get any worse, we're doomed."

"But in a good cause."

Through the storm the plane raced. Suddenly the motor died with sickening suddenness.

"Our haywire battery connections are gone," shouted McCready. "Say your prayers."

The wind tossed the plane about like a feather. Rapidly it lost altitude. A building loomed up before them. As a crash seemed imminent, a gust of wind caught the plane and tossed it up into the air again. For several minutes the ground could not be seen through the rain. Suddenly the plane hit an airpocket and dropped like a stone. With a splash it fell into the sea. A rift came for a moment in the curtain of rain.

"Look!" cried Carnes.

A hundred yards away, the *Denver* rode at anchor.

"I'm only sorry about one thing," said Carnes ten minutes later as they changed to dry clothes aboard the battle cruiser, "and that is that Saranoff wasn't in the factory when that salvo fell on it."

"I'm glad he was away," replied Dr. Bird. "With him absent, we succeeded in destroying it. If he had been there, our task would have been more difficult and perhaps impossible. I am an enemy of Saranoff's, but I don't underrate his colossal genius."